# PANDAMONIUM

# PEEK ZOO

For Helen and Kevin,

love,
KEVIN

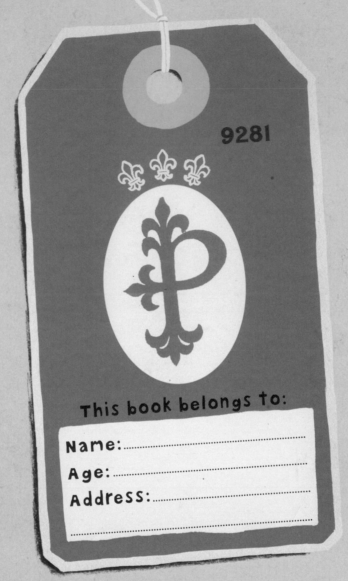

9281

This book belongs to:

Name: ..............................................

Age: ..............................................

Address: ..............................................

..............................................

A TEMPLAR BOOK

First published in the UK simultaneously in hardback
and paperback in 2013 by Templar Publishing,
an imprint of The Templar Company Limited,
Deepdene Lodge, Deepdene Avenue,
Dorking, Surrey, RH5 4AT, UK
www.templarco.co.uk

Copyright © 2013 by Kevin Waldron

First edition

ISBN 978-1-84877-285-4 (hb)
ISBN 978-1-84877-857-3 (pb)

Printed in China

# PANDAMONIUM
## AT
# PEEK ZOO

## BY
## KEVIN
## WALDRON

**templar** publishing

A **NEW PANDA** has been born at Peek Zoo!
Mr Peek the zookeeper and his son Jimmy
are busy making her feel at home.

Her name is **LULU** and she is a V.I.P. —
a **VERY IMPORTANT PANDA!**

Mr Peek decides to hold
a **SPECIAL EVENT**
to celebrate.

**51 PACES**

Mr Peek loves to daydream
about the animal parade.

"How heavenly it will be:
animals marching through the zoo
in perfect straight lines – everything
in apple-pie order."

The night before the big day, Mr Peek prepares a to-do list.

1. Feed giraffes
2. Feed penguins
3. Check gecko tank
4. Check polar bear pool
5. Clean elephants
6. Clean turtles
7. Feed monkeys
8. Feed pandas

Early the next morning, he steps out proudly
in his bottle-green uniform with Jimmy by his side.

They share the jobs between them.

"Oh gosh! We've forgotten to add 'Feed the lion' to the list!
Leave that to me, " says Mr Peek. "Mr Whiskerwitz will not
be forgotten. Jimmy my boy, it's all
tickety-boo at Peek Zoo!"

First Jimmy feeds Angela and Egbert, the two giraffes —
though he needs a little help to lock the door.

Meanwhile Mr Peek
feeds the penguins —

POOL AREA
KEEP GATE
CLOSED!

but he forgets to shut the gate.

Jimmy checks the temperature in the geckos' tank. Little Harold helps him record the figures in his daily report.

Mr Peek does the same for the polar bear... but he is not paying proper attention.

Jimmy washes Eleanor and her baby elephants...
and they provide a handy car wash!

Mr Peek polishes the tortoises, but he's in a bit of a rush.

"Must hurry, Horace!
Lots to do!"

Jimmy knows how to keep the monkeys happy.
He feeds them lots of bananas so they are ready
to entertain the crowds.

Mr Peek feeds the pandas
their bamboo, then hurries off
to take care of Mr Whiskerwitz...
perhaps a little **TOO** quickly.

It's only **NOW**, as he almost trips over a flapping flipper, that Mr Peek spots his black and white band of followers...

though he doesn't notice **ALL** of them...

"Dash it!
How did you lot get here?"

"Come along Jimmy! Help me get
these chaps home will you?
Hurry up everyone!
Follow me now.
Frightfully sorry, Mr Whiskerwitz.
I'll have to feed you later."

Hippo

Penguins

ars

Lion

oos

But not **EVERYONE** follows Mr Peek...

On his way back to the penguin pool,
Mr Peek realises that all is **NOT** well.

The tortoises are an unusual colour,
poor Kenneth is sweating,
and **WORSE STILL**...

**LULU IS MISSING!**

"APPLE SAUCE!
This is a DISASTER! Where can she be?"

Mr Peek races about, but the panda cub
is nowhere to be seen.

Meanwhile, visitors begin to arrive at the gates.

Mr Peek arrives back at the penguin pen
just as the zoo clock chimes nine.

"Hurry up! In you go!
We've got a panda to find."

There's no way the zoo can open in such a state.
The situation calls for an emergency
**PEEK PLAN OF ACTION.**

Jimmy is quick to act...

he spruces up the tortoises' shells...

He cools Herbert down with plenty of ice...

and he has everything back in apple-pie order
before you can say hipp-o-pot-a-mus!

But there is still one thing left for him to do...

At the same time, Mr Peek braves the waiting
public with the Peek Plan of Action **MASTERSTROKE**:

"Welcome to Peek Zoo! We have a special prize today
for the first visitor to spot the baby panda!"

He opens the gates...

and herds of humans flock into the zoo.

"Crumbs! You're keen."

A little girl is the first to find Lulu
and the crowds gather round.
But when Mr Peek scrambles to his feet
to see for himself, he **FREEZES**.

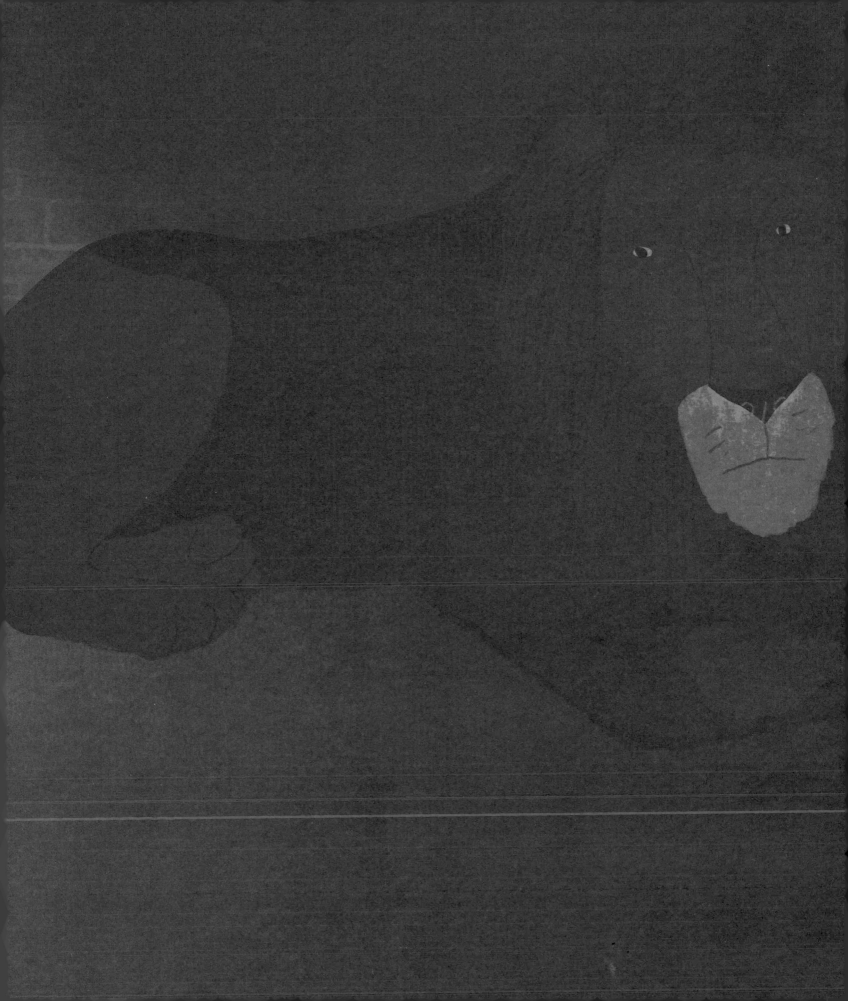

"Gadzooks! Lulu's in the lion's den –
and I forgot to feed him!

It's going to be

PANDAMONIUM!"

But even the really wild beasts are on friendly terms with Jimmy.

"Not to worry, Dad. I've fed Mr Whiskerwitz."

ROAR
For hungry lions

It seems there's nothing Mr Whiskerwitz likes more than a good play...

"PHEW!"

and he is as gentle as a lamb with the panda cub.

It's the perfect time to start the big event:

Ladies and Gentlemen
BOYS & GIRLS
PEEK  ZOO
PROUDLY PRESENTS
THE EVENT OF A LIFETIME
LET THE

ANIMAL
PARADE
begin
!!!

After a **LONG DAY**, father and son take a well-deserved rest.

WET PAINT

"Just like I said, all is tickety-boo at Peek Zoo!"
sighed Mr Peek happily.

Well, most of the time anyway!

Mr Peek's dream comes true:
animals marching in perfect
straight lines; everything
in apple-pie order; not a
**SLIP UP** in sight...

# The Daily

## BEST ZOO EVENT EVER!

Hundreds of residents took advantage of the summer skies to make yesterday the busiest day on record for Peek Zoo. Crowds flocked to see the new baby panda, Lulu, and they were not disappointed when zookeeper Mr Peek created a fantastic competition to start the day. Violet Henfrey, aged 8, won the prize for spotting Lulu — in the lion's cage of all places! Mr Peek thrilled the crowds as Lulu and the lion played happily — clearly the zookeeper is a master of his trade. Violet will name the next baby born at Peek Zoo and rumour has it that Mr Peek will win a prize for his magnificent showmanship. himself Peek zoo is home to animals from nearly temperate region of the world, and a tall order to create the right reature. Giraffes can't while penguins keepers